OUT
OF
FOCUS

OUT OF FOCUS

BY
ALF MACLOCHLAINN

THE DALKEY ARCHIVE PRESS

First published in Ireland in 1977 by the O'Brien Press

FIRST AMERICAN EDITION 1985

Book design / Michael O'Brien

Printed on acid-free paper

Library of Congress Catalogue Number: 85-072481
ISBN: 0-916583-13-9 softbd
0-916583-12-0 hardbd

Published with the assistance of the Illinois Arts Council

Printed in the United States of America

THE DALKEY ARCHIVE PRESS
1817 79th Avenue
Elmwood Park, IL 60635

Preface

My thanks are due to the Gesamthochschule, Kassel, to the University of Salamanca and to Loyola University, Chicago, who aided this work by unwittingly giving me the use of their stationery.

My wife did not do any of the typing and remains convinced that the whole thing is a complete waste of time.

A. Mac L.

Contents

Epigraph

"I assert first, that we do see all objects in two places ... the mind or visive faculty takes no notice ... From hence this paradoxical corollary arises: that an object may be seen in two places yet not seen double."

– William Molyneux, 1692.

1

Awake for Morning Looking Through the Alice Glass

I KNEW THAT I HAD BEEN asleep though not for long enough. The eye-sockets had the seared feeling of having been rebored for insertion of red-hot threaded bolts; the carapace of the head burned with the tightness of a metal helmet shrunken on like the rim of a wooden wheel and rivetted into place. Some of the heat had trickled down into the sticky mouth. There is a deep valley of real sleep but this I had obviously failed to penetrate, flitting instead on the scorching uplands of an unsatisfactory nap.

I kept my eyelids firmly clamped down and reached for the switch controlling the electric light on my bedside table. It had always been my experience that suffused pink light via the eyelids was a gentle introduction to full illumination. The switch clicked but no pinkness hit the eyeballs. The bulb, I knew, was ancient and probably defective. Old-fashioned clear bulbs, however, can have their ruptured filaments rejoined under favourable conditions. One of these conditions, of course, is enough light to do the job and there remained therefore the problem of getting the first light gracefully onto the eyeball. I put my hand out towards the string controlling the laced folding slat-built blind of the nearby window and pulled briefly. The slats turned obediently and the eyeballs gratefully acknowledged the dull pinkish glow. I slowly lifted one lid and then the other and found that the level of illumination was tolerable. Next I groped with my hand on the bedside table for my glasses, placed them on my nose and ears and happily cut off the fuzzy edges of the objects before me. Blinking once or twice

I shoved with my right index finger at the bridge of the glasses and they clicked finally into position.

I saw a group of girls at a distant corner. One was standing by her bicycle, two others tugged playfully at the handlebars and saddle respectively. Their schoolbooks, strapped into neat bundles, lay on the ground at their feet. Younger girls might have used schoolbags, the more studious small attaché cases. These were clearly, by their demeanour and accoutrements, girls in a slack school year between their intermediate and final examinations. The two were playing at preventing the girl with the bicycle from going home while she played at wanting to go.

The cause of this confrontation between this resistible force and that movable object came into view around a corner, a group of boys also equipped with standard issue strappings of books, one smoking as per programme. The boys stopped about thirty yards from the girls, whose playful battle redoubled its intensity momentarily, then ceased as they giggled, blushed and pointed, their hands making gestures narrower than the widths of their shoulders so that the boys should not notice. The boys dutifully failed to notice and continued a heedless conversation on football, cars and tennis-club hops. This new confrontation of resistible force and movable objects, the boys and the girls, soon sought resolution and the two groups broke up with a slow disentangling, the other two girls leaving the one with her bicycle, calling back to her over their shoulders obscure appointments and instructions; the boys spread equally slowly apart, drifting in amorphous groups of one or perhaps two or so in all directions.

One moved more slowly than the others and was available when the girl with the bicycle discovered a soft tyre. She postponed mounting her machine and took a pump from its metal moorings. She attached the rubber connection to valve and pump and manipulated the pump-piston industriously for a few strokes. There was a loud pop as the connection burst asunder. She was staring helplessly at her bicycle when the boy approached. They spoke briefly and came to the conclusion that the soft tyre was beyond remedy; the boy took the handlebars of the bike and began to wheel it away for her. She fell into step beside him and in making a show of attempting to wheel it herself found her hand resting in the comfortable crook of his elbow. Chatting and strolling, they too disappeared round the distant corner.

My spectacles, a heavy set with frames known to the trade as library frames, had slipped slightly down my nose and needed adjustment. I suspected that a fine film of overnight perspiration on the as yet unwashed face was the cause of the slippage and removed them, placing them carefully on the bedside table to leave my hands free for the skin-wiping. I immediately noticed the table lamp and remembered that I had as yet done nothing about the repair to the bulb.

I wiped the skin of the bridge of my nose and respectacled myself, unsocketed the bulb and set to work. Twin tendrils of fine-spun coiled filament pendulated sadly towards the lowered pot-belly bulge of the lamp. If these ends were to be made to touch and the current made again to flow through them so touching, they would fuse and a new if shorter filament would be there to enjoy some further hours of happy burning. Dexterously and slowly I swung the globe from side to side, watching the dangling filament ends as they swayed now nearer, now farther apart. A touch and their coiled adhesiveness of surface held them together. Then to manipulate the lamp-socket so that I could re-insert the bulb without shaking, then to click the switch and my poor eyeballs started back aghast into their own private sockets. The lamp was now brighter than rated, the surge of power through its shorter filament showering off slightly more quanticles per millisecond than your everyday hundred-watt job.

This would shorten the expectation of life of this poor little filament but after all was I not giving it one crowded hour of glorious life if also an early age without a name? Suppose, indeed, I was to shorten the filament still further, would I not ultimately reach the shortest possible filament and the brightest possible light? Had I invented the photographic flash-bulb?

I switched off the light and allowed myself to sink back towards sleep but not quite so far as it. As my head rolled slightly, the side of my glasses, and the pillow, between them nipped my ear painfully and I jolted awake, the glasses slipping off.

The resultant fuzzed image of my room had several interesting features, more noticeable now that a brighter daylight was up and about in the street outside and finding its way through the slats of my blind. Near the foot of my bed, neatly screwed to the wall, was my mirror. Its rippled and bevelled edges gleamed opalescent with rims of red and green and soft interflowing fringes of yellow and blue, the discreet fractions remaining of the sun's morning delivery on its interstellar round.

Quintrillions of those quanticles, of brain-blistering miniatude, were being constantly disgorged from the sun, vomited out from its forced feeding of itself on itself. Exhausted after their journey, the pale few reached me. The rest had been lost on the way, snapped up by passing asteroids, planets, satellites and clouds, these last, when fed up with the whole operation, unloading the lot in gigantic discharges of hot white lightning, hell-flames from a heavenly body.

There was a flicker here of something reminding me of a dream in my fitful nap, a dimly-lit signpost pointing back the way I had come.

Not light nor fire nor thermal furnace. A street, dazzling golden yellow on one side, harsh black on the other, a jagged shadow's edge along the middle, the high sun glaring down over the scalloped edging of tiled roof. A blacker hole on the black side, doorway, dim stairway to an upper landing, a door to a gloomy room, light filtering from stairwell, corridor to a blacker hole, a windowless room, a bed. Through the wall, high above the bed, an oblong hole cut, to admit air from a passage which had in its turn no outlet to air or light. I am lying on the bed, eyes opened to the blackness, pupils distended catching the faint gleam of borrowed light. Suddenly a switch clicks, the oblong is illuminated, a greenish patch projects onto the farther wall. Voices, a foreign language, something about two people, the house being full. A cordial laugh. A throatier voice and another laugh. Silence, the switch clicks again, darkness. A girl's voice, dying away. I am in the shadow-bisected street again, flaring yellow sandstone walls under a glaring impartial sun.

Anyway, this was getting away from the morning's business; recollecting a dream is always difficult and always a waste of time; remembered imagined hopes and fears, the roughage of life's digestive tract, unnoticed by a body in the glow of health. I replaced my glasses.

By now there was sufficient light available to and through my eyes to render the whole operation of mending the bulb a waste of time. I wondered what time it was. I reached out for my watch, lying obediently on the bedside table near the base of the lamp, but the lamp-work must have shifted it, for my fingers pushed it over the edge and it fell to the floor. Cosmic justice seemed to require that a slowly waking person be spared this series of petty annoyances; patience and resignation were called into play. I inverted my upper torso patiently and resignedly over the edge of the bed and groped below. With the head inverted the glasses slipped again, but this time upwards, so to speak, that is towards the forehead and away from the socketed nosebridge. My fingers came up with the watch-glass, sadly detached from its parent body. I brought it up close to my face to see if it at least had escaped damage and as I peered at it was surprised to see through it

A ragged column of young cyclists passing at moderate speed along a country road. The police bye-law requiring that cyclists travel no more than two abreast was not being strictly observed, although there was a tendency, no more, among the group to remain loosely formed into bi-sexual couples. The members of the group had a mean age of about eighteen years and seven months. The ratio of males to females was 1/1.23 recurring. As some of both the boys and the girls wore no socks, the number of socks per leg was 0.73. Most of the boys were wearing open-necked short-sleeved shirts of pastel colours and grey flannel trousers held tight at the ankle by clips designed to prevent the trouser-legs from fouling and being fouled by the driving-chains of the machines. Most of the girls were wearing blouses similar to the boys' shirts and cotton skirts of the style known as dirndl, a word in the German language denoting a garment worn by peasant girls in Bavaria and Austria, held tight by a broad band at the waist, flaring out slightly and extending just below the knee. These were in bright reds and blues and greens. One or two of the girls were wearing slacks like those of the majority of the boys. Two of the boys and one of the girls were wearing shorts, and these three, at the head of the column, were riding bicycles with handlebars curving sharply downwards and with the capacity to alter the ratio of movement of the crank-wheel to freewheel by a mechanism of the dérailleur type.

The posture, plump proportions and vigorous leg-action of this leading girl drew attention to her prominent bust, which, it appeared, was not supported with the rigidity held to be conventional. Change in public taste was to determine quite a different convention and girls of her age and endowment would affect a so-called natural look, all protuberances on the bust being left evident. It would be perfectly simple to devise a simulation of such protuberances on supports which could be worn by girls not endowed by nature with the features this 'look' required and I had no doubt ingenious manufacturers of ladies' undergarments had marketed such apparatus. Riding a bicycle with dropped handlebars might however require, for the sustaining of the simulation of the 'look' a mobility of the bust not allowed by protuberance-fitted supports. They would need, then, some attachment of light springing around the bases to impart this mobility; if this in its turn were found distressing by the wearer, the whole complicated support could be confined by one of the more conventional type – and, I suddenly realised, so on.

Each bicycle carried a small package strapped to its handlebars or clipped to a carrier mounted behind the saddle or, in the case of a few of the girls, in a light basket mounted on the handlebars and dangling dangerously over the front wheel. Each of these packets contained materials for a light lunch and a raincoat or cape of rubberised cotton.

The sun was shining with a watery bright yellowness proper to springtime, St. Patrick's Day or Easter Monday.

The one girl I recognised was roughly three-quarters way back through the column and losing place steadily. She was still having trouble with her soft tyre. Her next neighbour was a boy, the only other recognisable member of the group, and he kept even pace with her as her disability dropped her farther and farther back. In his face were mingled distress (at allowing himself to be passed out by fellow-cyclists, boys and girls, whom he regarded as his inferiors in prowess) and self-satisfaction with the protective role he had assumed towards his companion.

The road was poorly paved and each patch of loose repair metal made the girl wince a little as her soft tyre bumped across it. It was such bumping and her consequent slackening of speed which were gradually driving her back. Finally, she and her

Schematic representation of cumulative effect of natural/non-natural bust supports. (Section at A-A).

escort had reached the end of the column and the now-penultimate couple glanced back as they passed with grins and facetious comment.

At the next bump, she applied her brakes and stopped. Her companion stopped beside her and the column swung ahead round a corner into a black cavernous opening in a tunnel of overhanging trees and out of sight.

A hammering of blood in my temples and behind my eyes forcibly reminded me that long hanging upside-down over the edge of a bed staring through a watch-glass becomes hurtful to several of the senses and could eventually inflict irreversible brain-damage. I drew myself up, the effort adding an aching wheeze in my head and lay back on my pillow.

Care of my eyesight particularly was most important to me, as the principal hobby to which I devoted my spare time was experimentation with the Alice-glass.

Head clear, skin dry, blinds open, I felt free to try again for the parent watch. I rationed my time strictly to avoid another attack of the bends; I reached over and stretched my arm as far under the bed as I could, covering a semi-circle of floor in a careful sweep; I was relieved to touch the lump of my watch on the first attempt.

I examined the dredge and observed that the mechanism, a circular assembly, had been jerked upwards in its tiny case, thus, presumably, dislodging the glass which I had already retrieved. A gentle shaking and tapping quickly caused the mechanism to fall back to the floor of its case and left room for the glass in its metal rim to fit back into its homely groove. To snap the glass on was the work of a deft moment but its homeward click was instantaneously followed by a faint assertive buzzing. The hands of the watch were spinning around at about sixteen hours to the minute. The train was in order but the fine hair-spring for checking it to normal dispensation of time was clearly disarboured, adrift and useless.

Time, too, is a measure of the spraying energy of the self-consuming sun, by year, season and day. To store this energy might save time, but it cannot unfortunately be stored in any readily usable form. The capture by clouds of stray fragments of solar discharge and their subsequent erratic release in lightning has already been noted. Layers of fine droplets capture a little but pass it on immediately in the form of coloured light or rainbow. More controlled methods of capture and release certainly deserve study.

For many centuries scientists from Leonardo on had been aware of the power of a black hole to harness the passing rays from the sun into patterns on the inner wall of a camera obscura. The introduction of a lens merely extended the range of control of the incident by-product of the solar furnace. A useful but intellectually disquieting side-effect was the ability of the glass (or the black hole) to work on light other than that of solar origin. The atomic explosion at Trinity site, for example, had produced volumes of light so intense as to pierce holes in the photographic plates exposed to it. The process by which initial exposure produces a negative image is known to every schoolboy but who could determine whether these Trinity site holes in the plates were black holes or white holes?

The problem of relating solar fire and solar time remained. Extending the photographic process in time gave at least a hint of the theoretical basis of the kinematograph.

Part of the soligneous detritus impinges on the subject of a photograph and is reflected via the objective lens onto the sensitive layer of the plate. Note that the subject is bombarded by the rays to be reflected whether the reflected rays are captured by a camera or not. If they are not captured, some at least will be returned to the subject by surrounding surfaces. If they are captured they are lost forever to the subject. Now this bombardment is in no sense a merely notional event: real energeticules of the brain-blistering miniatude noted above can be compared on a trans-microscopic scale to the sand blasting at a smoke-blackened building. Examine the heap which accumulates at the foot of a sand-blasted wall. It contains the sand, certainly, and each grain of the sand carries with it some of the blackness it has dislodged from the wall-surface. In similar fashion, tiny fragments of me are lodged in the photographic plate each time a photograph is taken of me. The physical loss to me, it will be acknowledged, is negligible; but consider the sad fate of the film-star. He is subjected to this subnuclear auto-da-fé twenty-four times a second every time the camera is turned on him. Perhaps the loss will become appreciable, even though the greater part of his body is protected by clothes. Consider his sister performer, condemned by modern taste to appear much of the time before the camera with little or no protective clothing, the skin-flick-knives of solar and artificial incandescence tearing her away, flensing her down until layer after layer of her has been stolen and mounted in frame after frame of the miles of film exposed in front of her. And worse. When it is intended to show her naked posturings in what is called slow motion, it is necessary to double the number of pictures taken of her in each second so that the pictures taken in one second will take two seconds to be projected before the audience, and pro rata for increasing slowness. Further, a picture exposed for only one hundredth of a second requires twice the amount of light required for a picture exposed for a fiftieth. Any wonder therefore that so many of the beautiful girls exposed before cine-cameras fade away like the morning dew under the pitiless sun?

Thus erosion year by year, in season and out, down to the day and a half my frantic watch had spun past me in a couple of solar minutes.

There is a clear theoretical connexion between glass lens, glass plate giving negative mirror image and glass mirror. Momentarily I glanced at my mirror hanging as noted near the foot of my bed.

Soft greens were in focus there, curling fronds of bracken, waving tall grass. In the foreground a pale-green blouse and a dark-green shirt, on the girl and the boy tending the stricken bicycle. As they leaned together over it, their shoulders touched, the boy turned his head quickly and kissed his companion on the cheek. She turned her head and returned the quick kiss, then pulled away slightly and laughingly indicated that they should get on with the job.

Their mingled hands pulled the cover from the slack tube and palping and pulling it they paused inch by inch to inspect, finding at last the tiny black hole. A hard rubbing cleared the area around it; a small rubber disc was peeled and laid ready; a quick squirt placed a jet of sticky solution on the cleared area; a pause gave it time to become tacky; the peeled rubber disc was placed on the tacky area over the hole and pressed home with the thumb; another pause to allow the work to dry off; talc was grated around repair to prevent adhesion to cover.

Diligent pumping hardened the tube again and the hole remained successfully sealed. They deflated the tube by removing the valve, manipulated it under the cover, carefully checking there was no pinching, replaced valve, pumped again, returned the machine to its erect position, stowed lunch and raincoat and rode away.

There was no fundamental difference between the processes used for the production of glass for mirrors, photographic plates, lenses, bulbs, stout-bottles or crystal balls. Sands of certain chemical composition are placed in a suitable furnace and fused by fire of fierce but appropriate heat into runny and ductile gobs of molten stuff of one sort or another.

I had tried crystal gazing myself but with little success. As I had sat staring at the transparent sphere I had noticed that each passing cloud, each vehicle passing on the road outside, had caused a distorted image of itself to swirl grotesquely around the surface of my ball. I had closed the shutters and blinds to cut out this interference and found that I could see nothing at all. I then tried with stable artificial light and discerned in the glass a horrid idiot image of my own face, the mouth slobberingly expanded, the nose slanting back to retracted pinpoint eyes. Moving the head to produce a less distracting image merely distributed the distortion among the several features more or less unfavourably. As for seeing the past or the future of the character of myself or any other, absolutely nothing, just a black hole.

It is said that contemplative elderly people sitting snugly staring at an open fire on a dark winter evening can see in the dancing flames the figurations of distant friends and relatives, people dead and gone, time running back to imaginings of youth and springtime, pink spectacularisations of the past.

My other lightsome sphere, the sun, might do as much for me. My spectacles might serve poorly and barely adequately for its examination. I was not such a fool as to stare at the sun through a lens, every child's manual of primitive astronomy warns against it. I manipulated the slats of my blind to provide some kind of black hole approximating to the aperture of a pinhole camera. The sun was now high enough to have an uninterrupted trajectory into my room. A bright spot was cast upon the pillow-slip near my head; I took the spectacles from

SHOT  PROOF

CRYSTAL EYE PROTECTORS.

THE EYE PROTECTORS are without "power," but may be adapted to the sight of the Wearer without difficulty, as the Pebbles can be worked to any focus. The Steel Frames are Nickel-Plated to avoid rust. Sides and fronts are made in Brazilian Pebble $\frac{5}{16}$-inch thick. Price £3 13s. 6d. nett.

COUNTY CLUB, CARLISLE,
February 26th 1898.

DEAR SIRS,—I duly received your letter about my shooting shields and think it will be best to have the nickel frames, as I always had great difficulty in keeping them free from rust before. I cannot speak too highly of the glasses. I have worn them for a good many years now and don't know what I should do without them. They are a positive comfort on a wild day's grouse driving; they protect the eyes completely from wind and storm. I have been shot twice in the face since wearing them, but have not the least nervousness as I have such implicit confidence in the glasses for protecting my eyes. You are at perfect liberty to make any use of this letter you care to, as I consider them the greatest boon a shooting man with short sight could possibly go in for.

Yours faithfully,
JOHN K. PARKER.

Messrs. CARPENTER & WESTLEY,
24 Regent Street, London, W.

CARPENTER AND WESTLEY,
Opticians,
24 REGENT STREET, WATERLOO PLACE,
LONDON, S.W.

the nose and inserted them in the path of this incoming light, hoping to cast on my pillow a focussed image of the sun which I could examine at leisure.

Certainly a more or less round bright disc appeared. Without my spectacles I could not determine exactly whether or not it was clearly defined at the edges. I moved my glasses up and down in the path of the incident beam; the disc grew brighter and sharper as the glasses approached a critical point. I held them there and was horrified to see a tiny wisp of smoke emerge from my pillow-case. I jerked away the glasses and beat out the small glowing spot of burning I had caused, leaving only a browned area with a tiny black hole in the middle.

Here at least was another capture of solar energy. I began to worry about the possible exhaustion of this energy and to devise means for conserving it and restoring it to its source. Heal the drought of Africa by poising over it in the stratosphere a gigantic hemispherical mirror which would return directly to the sun the incident light captured by this mirror. Thereby we could extend the life of the solar system, refuel the sun with its own excrement. It must by magnetic attraction recapture some of this anyway. As it recycles its own effluent, is this in a coarse and clinical meaning a case of perpetual motion?

If the sun were to recover it all would it swell like the ugly pumped frog of cruel boys and burst as a super-nova, dazzling for a moment and scattering itself in all directions, leaving nothing at the original centre but a black hole? If the quantities it attracts are not as great as those it disgorges, will it shrink at an accelerating rate and finish as a black lump without even the compensation of the crowded hour of glorious life enjoyed by the exploding supernova? I was reminded of the shortened filament of my electric bulb and glanced over at it. How stupid I had been to waste hours of sea-shore searching in my youth for a green glass net-float to use as a gazing crystal. The pot-bellied bulge of my lamp would have done just as well, indeed could not have done worse. I looked more closely at the bulb. The part-drawn slats of the blind cast strange shadows on it, perhaps of shining reflective surfaces outside in the street, but somehow more familiar.

The boy and the girl were there again, sitting together on a park bench. They were snugly close, shoulder to shoulder and

Dandelion-clock with calibration for sidereal time comparison.

hand in hand but there was no passion in their posture of state rather than imminent action. They were silent for a stretch of minutes. Then they exchanged some grinning shy words; the boy slipped his hand into his pocket and withdrew a tiny wrap of tissue paper. He took his other hand from hers and with mock-gravity of ceremony he unfolded the tissue to reveal a slim gold ring set with a cluster of small stones. The centre stone was an opal, its interior facets flaring and glinting brown and gold and green as the ambient sunlight caught it or the heat of the hand altered its luminosity. It was set amidst four tiny diamonds, the ancient distillation of the primordial fire of the world.

The girl held out her acquiescent left hand, struggling to deflect the first, second and fourth fingers while she held the third erect. The boy's fondling hand gently brushed down the length of the finger, pushing the ring, its stones twinkling and gleaming. It slipped over her second knuckle and stopped. His hand squeezed hers and quickly he put his other arm around her shoulder and they kissed.

I decided it was time to get up.

2

On a Strangely Synchronous Afternoon

AS I NOW RECALL, I should have realised early that it was a strangely synchronous day. Walking down the street that morning I strode quickly along close to the wall, my usual practice, and on turning a corner came face to face with another man of the same espalier habit. I slackened speed and shuffled slightly sideways, beginning a half-smile of self-deprecation, embarrassment and apology. My protagonist followed like a mirror image my every shuffle and grin, slipping to his right as I slipped to the left, to his left as I altered course to starboard, and we finished eyeball to eyeball, rotating slowly as we moved through matched arcs of one hundred and eighty degrees, figures in an antique dance.

A few minutes later I undertook the crossing of a one-way street. Before stepping off the pavement I glanced both right and left, trusting no-one, and descried a single motor-car approaching at moderate speed in the permitted direction. The street was otherwise free of traffic and I stepped forward onto the roadway, moving slowly to allow the motorist time to drive past before I should reach any point on his planned path. The motorist, however, perhaps attributing my slowness to infirmity and anxious to extend courtesy to the disabled, reduced speed and wagged his head in token that I should have precedence in use of the road. Noting his reduced speed but having no knowledge of the reasons for it – perhaps mechanical failure, perhaps excess of caution, perhaps the charitable motive suggested above – I decided to adopt a pace more normal for my years and strength and marched boldly forward. The motorist now, seeing perhaps that a gesture of courtesy had been misplaced and imagining in his turn that the few feet of roadway I had traversed left him still generous room for passing without danger to either of us, accelerated. Rapid consideration left me convinced that his previous retardation and my having pushed forward into the traffic-way together left me in a position to complete the traverse before he could reach me, and I accordingly speeded up my walk still further to make sure of safety; but his continuing acceleration rendered collision a distinct possibility so I again slackened speed only to note that he, placing the same interpretation on the data available to us mutually, had also slowed down. It was now a matter of unwilling bluff and double-bluff, two movable objects in the grip of a ridiculous but irresistible force and we proceeded by a series of stop-go accelerations, slowings-down and head-waggings until the front wing of his car, almost at a stand-still, struck me on the thigh. I had barely steerage way but unfortunately tripped and fell, striking my back heavily on the ground.

The motorist was solicitous in the extreme and insisted on taking me to hospital for a full assessment of my condition and on informing my next of kin.

Normally, to peer at your feet you peer downwards, but one lying flat on his back and peering at his feet can only be described as peering along or across at them. This I did, with some difficulty, as the bruises on my back made even the slight head-movement required fairly strenuous. There the feet were, evidenced by two ridged prominences in the snowy wastes of the bed-spread. Couloirs, cwms and crevasses shuddered and changed shape as I waggled my toes. Next, I carefully flexed one knee, thus bringing its foot, one would have presumed, nearer to my head than the other foot. The presumption was borne out by optical evidence collated in the course of the elaborate ensuing experiment. Continuing to peer in the general direction of the feet, I closed an eye briefly and as it re-opened closed the other, equally briefly, repeating the procedure a number of times, left, right, left, right. The left- and right-eyed view-points presented quite different bed-scapes. Left eye surveyed (reading from left to right) left foot, right foot and right knee. Right eye saw only left foot and raised knee, the knee occluding or eclipsing the right foot. So far so good. I straightened the knee again, reproducing the earlier configuration. I was then disturbed to find that further closings and openings of the eyes failed to produce any significant alteration in the occlusions of the remoter landscapes behind (hardly below) the feet. As the opposite wall of the ward was, like the bedspread, of a neutral tinge, it was not possible to establish coordinates which would be of any use to me in determining the length of my legs, or even, indeed, if they were of the same length. A smart lateral striking together of the balls of the great toes, while both knees were straight, disposed of the amendment to the motion, but even if the legs were of the same length, was that length twelve inches or twelve feet or even perhaps as many miles?

My planning of further experiments in optical orientation and leg-measurement was interrupted by the arrival of a nurse, who told me a young lady had rung up to say she would try to get in on the afternoon train to see me.

I resented the suggestion that a few bruises on the back called for such elaborate arrangements 'to see me'.

'Would you like a bath?' the nurse asked.

Indeed I would and a few minutes later I was standing alone in my pelt in a narrow bathroom. The nurse with some misgiving had finally accepted my assurance that I could look after myself.

I leant with both hands for security on the side of the bath, the conventional enamelled type, about five feet long and two feet wide. I was standing beside one of its longer sides, a short side equipped with twin taps to my right, the sloping and curved short side, fitted for accommodating human backs, to my left.

Considerable planning would be necessary, I realised. My real, if slight and temporary, disablement required the avoidance of the necessity for sudden and violent movement. Hence I must not attempt to enter a bath already full of water which might prove too hot for comfort. It seemed logical to me therefore that I should enter the bath at my leisure while it was still empty and control the inflow of hot and cold supply in such fashion that comfort was assured. A rapid glance around confirmed access to soap, sponge and towel and ignoring the steps which hospitals thoughtfully supply I stepped easily over the side, turned on the hot tap, and sat down.

Initial hot inflow is subject to perceptible heatloss through the warming of the metal of the bath (specific heat 1.03 recurring). A nice adjustment is necessary of this first inrush, the gradual lowering of the thighs against the bottom of the bath proving an excellent test for the even heating of the highly conductive steel sheeting.

At the critical moment, my hands reached out to grasp hot and cold taps, ready to reduce hot delivery and allow cold. Again, so far so good. An even and comfortable temperature was being maintained, depth was increasing at a satisfactory rate, I could sit back, straighten my legs (memo: measure bath to establish length of legs), lay my spine, still a little sensitive, to the sloped area at the back and survey the gradual rise of the water-surface. As the water crept up the side of the bath I noted the delicate meniscus of the interface. Ankle-knobs disappeared, water lapped about the knee-caps.

Suddenly a distant clashing was heard, followed by the mingled hiss, gurgle and rattle of water being drawn from some remote central cistern. The cold tap faltered, gargled, spat and revived, but its delivery-rate had slackened noticeably. Unless corrective measures were undertaken as a matter of urgency, temperature would alter perceptibly upwards. I reached forward again towards the taps, but too quickly and the muscles of my back convulsed. Unnerved, I had to hang for a moment on the two taps. I twisted the hot one slightly, reducing its flow successfully and quickly let go as it was too hot for comfortable touching. I rested then with both hands on the cold tap and found my face close to an interesting orifice placed in the wall of the bath between the taps. It was in the shape of a miniature rose window and from its centre a light chrome chain connected with the rubber stopper sealing the vent-hole in the floor of the bath.

I recognised the orifice as an overflow, though any somnolent or otherwise inactive reclining bather would be well drowned before the engulfing water would reach its threshold. Consideration for damaged floors, ceilings, plaster and wall-paper, if not for a few drowned patients, should have made the designers place this orifice at least a foot lower. My ear was near it and I could hear, super-imposed on the gurgling of my two taps, a distant quiet sizzling. I turned my head to bring eye rather than ear to bear on the rose window and was surprised to notice a distinct if tiny glow emanating from its interior. My back was by now accommodated to its position and I could move fairly freely. I brought my eye close to the hole and peered in.

The view was in part obscured by the metal rays or spokes of the rose-window pattern but the details of the high-angle distant prospect were unmistakable: she was getting off a train. Good heavens, I thought, can it be so late already?

She stood on the platform, glancing up and down in indecision. She was carrying in her right hand a medium-sized travelling-case. Its medium size was plainly the cause of her indecision. A large bag would have required the assistance of a porter or of one of the silently-running articulated luggage-trolleys supplied by Messrs. Northern Engineering, Gateshead, of which several were to be seen whirring up and down the station. A small bag she would unhesitatingly have taken with her at a brisk walk. As it was, most of the passengers had preceded her to the exit when at last she emerged and approached the one remaining taxi. The driver, sitting at the wheel, was hunched over a newspaper. She spoke to him.

'Can you take me to the City Hospital, please?'

She elicited no response. She spoke again and he looked up with an annoyed frown, then with a twist of the lips and a wave of his hand dismissed her. The newspaper before him was folded neatly to expose a diagram presenting a two-move chess problem hinging on a promotion risking stale-mate.

Water was rising to operational levels so I withdrew my head from the vicinity of the rose window and in gingerly consideration for my back retreated along the bath, checking, before leaving, that the cold tap had returned to normal delivery. The water I found on reaching the full-back position and stretching out was now comfortably deep and hot and with two swift left-ward swipes of the right toes I closed off both hot and cold taps (memo: further evidence of leg-length) but not so firmly that toes would be unable to reopen them.

Cogitate as I might I could find no explanation for the light emanating from the overflow nor for the strange view it afforded of relatively distant places. So far there was no evidence that distant times too were being brought under my gaze for it was perfectly in order that she should at that particular moment be dismounting from a train at a city terminal.

The unnecessary height of the overflow above the bath floor I had already noticed. Several other practical aspects of the matter required review. What of those baths, admittedly not nowadays so frequently met with, which combine overflow and vent-hole-stopper in a single metal tube, which fits into the vent-hole and effectively prevents escape of water until drawn up by means of a neat piston-like handle marked 'pull' set midway between the two taps? Such tubes function as overflows by having their upper ends open, the 'pull' handle being attached to a diametrical bar across the upper end. Taps and 'pull' handle on a bath so fitted must be set in a wide lip overhanging the interior of the bath. It would be quite impossible for the bather to insert his head beneath this lip and above the sealing-tube. *A fortiori* it would be quite impossible for him or her to determine whether or not such an overflow was acting as light-trap, periscope and telescope, and indeed the tubular structure of such overflows might lead to appreciably improved performance as all three.

Ratiocination on these and associated lines of enquiry occupied my mind for a considerable time and a minor water-reheating operation had to be undertaken. I reached my left foot out and up and grasped the lugs of the hot tap carefully (memo: note leg-length), engaging the knuckle of the great toe about a lug pointing so to speak towards four o'clock, that is considering the inscribed 'H' on a red ground on top of the tap as clock-centre. My no. 2 toe was inserted behind a lug pointing to eight o'clock and made to exert a supporting pressure. The tap obediently delivered water, cool at first but almost immediately hot enough to rewarm my bath. Enquiringly I attempted at the same time to engage the cold tap with my right foot but found to my surprise that it was extremely difficult to turn the two taps in the same direction at the same time. The attempt to do so involved a multiplying torque reaching, by the linkage of my legs, the sensitive areas of my spine. To turn hot on and cold off at the same moment was perfectly simple. The pressures required were in fact equal and opposite, half-torque was balanced by counter-vailing half-torque and spine was left unmolested; but only hot water was delivered. I had perforce to turn off the hot tap but already my right toes, still hooked on the cold tap, had acquired a Pavlovian reflex and carried out an involuntary movement in the opposite direction. Filing away the perplexing results of this experiment I decided that manual overdrive was called for in the interests of my spine, recalled my legs and reached forward with my two hands to the taps. This concatenation of movements again brought my head into the vicinity of the tiny rose window.

'Hanging about' is the only word to describe her behaviour. She wandered a few steps forward and back, near the rear of the single taxi with its immobile chess-playing driver. She put down her bag, picked it up again, looked back towards the railway-platform, over towards the exit leading to the city, put down her bag, bit her nail meditatively, made small erratic gestures with her shoulders and head. Two boys were sitting on the sun-baked pavement by the taxi-rank. She glanced at them, peered farther afield, then returned her gaze to them. They were playing jack-stones*; and one of them was approaching the climax.

He examined the five pebbles lying on the ground, carefully appraising their dispersal, their several rotundities and angularities, and his mind made up, quickly picked one up, tossed it in the air and as it sailed up shot his hand with lightning speed across the group of four left on the ground, sweeping them

---

*This game can be either an exercise of skill and patience for an individual or a contest between two. The skill and patience are exploited in prescribed manipulations of five small stones or pebbles, each about the size of the top joint of a little finger. Participants sit or squat upon the ground, a level area of a few feet square being required, free from extraneous pebbles or vegetation. A city pavement is an admirable location.

The stones are dropped from the hand onto the ground so that they lie within a compass of a few inches. Competitor A (let us say) commences. He takes one of the pebbles, tosses it in the air and allows it to land on the back of his hand. If he is successful he tosses it from the back of his hand and catches it in his palm. If he fails to catch at any point his right to continue play lapses and his rival begins. If A has been successful in the two stages of his work with the single stone, he proceeds, tossing it again in the air and *while it is aloft grabbing a second stone from those lying on the ground* and then catching the first as it descends. He now tosses the two stones which are in his palm and tries to catch them on the back of his hand; if he succeeds he tosses them from the back of the hand and catches them on the palm; and further proceeding tosses the two,

into his clutching palm in time to switch his hand back, turn and open it just as the first tossed stone arrived to join its fellows safely on the palm. He sighed briefly with relief, allowing the five stones to cradle themselves comfortably in his curved fingers. He had now to launch these upwards in as tight a formation as possible and allow them to land on the back of his hand. A smooth rising glide of the hand, with his fingers forming an upward-pointing funnel, shot them gently in the air; his hand flicked over following them, descended below them just as they began to fall, wavering with spread knuckles as they spread slightly in their fall until one, two, three, four, five had clicked safely home as his hand came to rest without a tremor not an inch from the ground. The game was almost over. It only remained for him to toss the five now safely ensconced on the back of his palm. He tossed and grabbed and a vicious click told that one of the stones had knocked another. It knocked it three or four feet away and he was left with the useless four in his hand which put him back to the very beginning again. At this point the girl asked him would he carry her bag for her.

I began to fear that the nurse might return soon and expect to find me with my ablutions completed. Crouched as I was at the tap end of the bath I had several options open to me. I could

---

grabs a third and so on.

When he has successfully tossed and grabbed all up to and including the fifth he progresses to grabbing two at a time, then two and three, then four and then five. Competitors of international class have further requirements added; the falling stone must not be allowed to make a click against those already in the palm, for example. Initial choice of pebbles is clearly a matter of grave import. Pebbles which are too rounded will roll too easily from the back of the hand, those which are too flat are difficult to grab quickly from the ground. Mathematicians might tentatively express the game in some such form as $T(1\rightarrow5)G[(1\rightarrow(1+4)]$ where 'T' means 'toss' and 'G' means 'grab'.

The foregoing summary gives little idea of the skill and competitive spirit which may be engaged in so seemingly simple a game. One of the two boys mentioned above had reached the penultimate and critical point at which he was faced with the problem of grabbing four stones from the ground and thereafter tossing five from the back of the hand (T5G4 in the notation suggested).

stay where I was, convenient to my peephole, and by a slight adjustment of knees, etc., assume the normal posture of one sitting on the ground, with my legs flat on the floor of the bath, my feet pointed towards the sloped end. There would be an undoubted if slight advantage in depth of water about the buttocks but the position was definitely at variance with the method of using the bath intended by the designers. As, however, I had already noted several design-faults in this bath, and indeed in baths in general, perhaps this was not even persuasive. I decided finally that sitting with my right and left shoulders in imminent danger of sharp contact with hot and cold taps respectively would be a gross perversion and eased myself into the designed position with my back to the slope. Now another design fault became apparent.

The soap was sitting in a small depression beside the hot tap and I could not reach it with my outstretched hand. It would be necessary to flex my knees, bringing my whole body forward, to leave the soap within range. A number of possible design improvements immediately occurred to me, some I knew already available through commercial outlets. First, the Bailey bridge type of soap-tray. This is a plastic or metal tray equal in length to the width of the bath. It is furnished with projecting moulded handles at both ends which sit firmly on the bath-rims. The tray provides adequate accommodation for face-cloths, sponges, if desired, soaps, light plastic containers for proprietary brands of shampoo, cubes of so-called bath salts of a mildly detergent character which impart a faint sliminess to the water, appreciated by some bathers. On the whole, one might think, a useful device; but profoundly inhibiting to pedal operation of taps as outlined above.

Floating soap might seem a solution to the accessibility problem and could be readily manufactured by the incorporation in each tablet of a vacant air-bubble. Decomposition of such tablets, permanently in contact with warm water, would inevitably be rapid and a point would soon be reached when the soap-skin would become perilously thin and finally pierced at one or more points. At that stage the soap would inevitably fill with water and sink. A floating and sealed soap-container then occurred to me and I rapidly sketched out in my mind a suitable design, lined with sponge or aerated plastic foam, consisting of two halves hinged together and held closed or open by springs easily tripped by pressure on external nodules.

Worthwhile exploitation of this device would require fitting it with some motive power and directional navigation remotely controlled to ensure its recovery from the farther (normally the tap) end of the bath, whither it might so easily drift under the impulsion of convection currents as the bath water changed temperature. Sophisticated miniaturised hardware, perhaps strapped to the head of the bather, seemed called for. The container could of course be fitted with a magnet and the bather equipped with a belt and anklets magnetised to appropriate polarities. Successive attractions and repulsions would drive the container in any required direction. Again, directional jets loaded with liquid soap could be placed at strategic points around the bath-rim.

Unfortunately time and material resources did not permit the execution of any or all of these projects and against the possible arrival of the nurse I felt the agonising need to act. I reached forward, flexing the knees to grasp the soap. To my dismay it refused to lift with my fingers. I tugged harder and was horrified when it finally gave, to hear a squelching, popping noise and to see attached to the bath a soap-retainer of yet another kind. It was a thin piece of rubber, flat, oval, three or four inches in its longer axis, two or three in its shorter, fitted on both surfaces with a large number of tiny suction-cups. When the device was pressed on a bath surface, even a vertical one, these cups adhered aggressively. A soap-tablet pressed upon the upper surface would now adhere equally closely and could be removed only by such tugging as would cause a large number of lacerated wounds on the soap surface.

It was soap so scarred that I held in my hand with some revulsion and I paused still crouched near the tap end. I noticed again the faint gleam in the over-flow hole.

The boy was hefting her case in his hand. It was certainly not too heavy for a man to carry, perhaps slightly uncomfortable for a girl, difficult for a twelve-year-old boy. His difficulty was compounded by the necessity to transport as well his bicycle, which was lying near where he had been playing with his friend. With the case in his right hand, he grasped the head of the bicycle with his left midway between the handlebars. He attempted to lift the machine but its centre of gravity was far

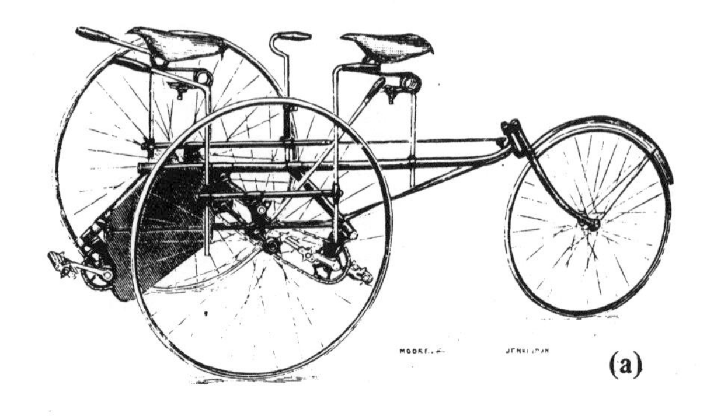

Alternative means (a) and (b) of cycle transport for carrying small travelling cases from main station to city hospital.

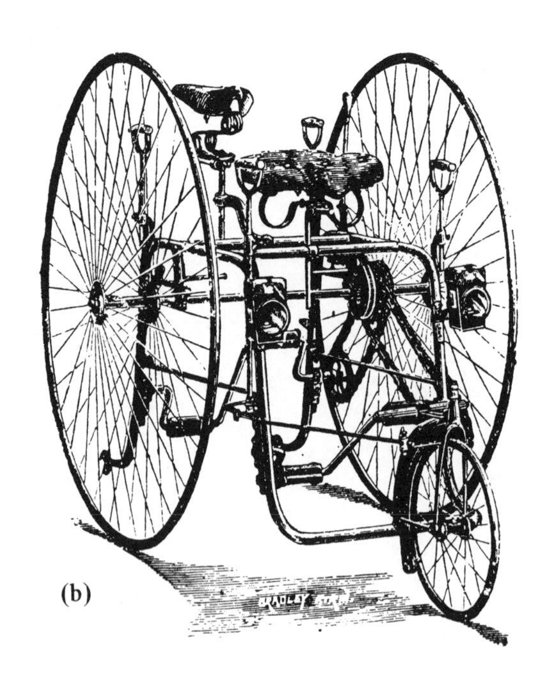

from his point of contact and the head twisted in his hand, the front wheel swivelling upwards, and the frame and rear wheel fell heavily to the ground. He relinquished his hold on the case, stood the bicycle up correctly and grasped the case again. As it left the ground and became part of his gravitational system his centre of gravity changed and he leant over in compensation. The bicycle slid downwards, its front wheel again twisting, rolling away from him, and the cross-bar slipping down along his thigh.

He released both bicycle and case, took the bicycle firmly, walked to a nearby wall and planted the bicycle firmly against it. Returning he took the case in his hands and brought it to the bicycle, then set about placing it carefully at a slant in the notional triangle formed by the front of the saddle, the cross-bar and the head. The case measured 15" x 24" x 4", was notably shallow that is to say for its height and length, and fitted but ill into the allotted place. Further, the eight points at which its six sides converged in corners were reinforced with metal shoes which gave to the whole a readiness to slide when these shoes came in contact with other metal surfaces.

Slowly and carefully, with his right hand on the right-hand handle-bar and his left steadyingly on the case, he piloted the bicycle away from the wall, propelling it by pressure on the rear portions of the saddle from the front of his left hip. He began to follow the girl. As they came to the exit proper from the station premises she stopped abruptly to check on approaching traffic before crossing the street. The boy stopped equally abruptly and the resultant jerk dislodged the case from its precarious emplacement. It slipped heavily sideways, coming to rest askew in the angle formed by the turning of the head-bar into the left handle-bar. The centre of gravity had again changed and the late attempt to establish equilibrium caused the case to slip formlessly to the ground on the farther side of the machine from the perplexed boy. Resourcefully he wheeled the bike in a long circle, so approaching the case as he came around that it was again convenient to his right hand. This time, he poised the case transversely on a small carrier behind the saddle, its lower 4" x 24" side (that is the narrow side opposite the handle), resting on the carrier, a light spring hinged at the back of the carrier exerting some pressure on the whole. In stable conditions the arrangement was ideal, but the centre of gravity was dangerously high and the transverse arrangement of the longer axis of the case gave little prospect of trouble-free locomotion. The potential danger became cruelly actual when the journey was recommenced. Bumping his bicycle off the pavement to follow the girl across the street, the boy again lost control of the machine, the case slipping sideways. He grabbed frantically at it, yet again altering the centre of gravity of the whole boy-bike-case system. The bike slid away from him, landing flat on its side and in the final inches of its fall dealing him a smart blow on the left ankle with its saddle. The involuntary spasm in his ankle plunged him into still further disequilibrium, and case, bike and boy finished in a sprawled heap on the roadway.

With the soap in my hand I had to decide which particular phase of the ablutions to undertake first. There would seem to be some linear logic in starting at either head or feet, but considerations other than mere linearity had to be borne in mind. There was bound to be substantial difference between the dirt-deliveries of head and feet. Justifiable objection might be made to rinsing the head in water already fouled by the off-scouring of perspiratory feet. On the other hand, the hair is a notable dust trap and washing it first would transfer a perceptible quantity of mechanical dirt and other atmospheric pollutants to the water. Again, the hands are notoriously the most efficient dirt-collectors of all the human members and many bathers would not be prepared to use them for working the other members until they themselves had been thoroughly washed and rinsed, even though such washing and rinsing would transfer to the water a quantity of dirt unreasonably out of proportion with the superficial area cleansed.

'Tisk, tisk,' said the nurse, sticking her head round the door, 'aren't you ready yet? I'll come back in a minute.'

Haste was necessary and as I had the soap in my hand I began there, lathering furiously. Feet, legs, buttocks, torso followed quickly and heedless of foot-sweat I plunged my head into the now-tepid water. As my ears breached the surface on the way down I was suddenly conscious of a distant altercation dimly heard. Undoubtedly sound travels more easily through water than through air but what frog-men in distant reservoir could be arguing so loudly that their querulous tones could reach me

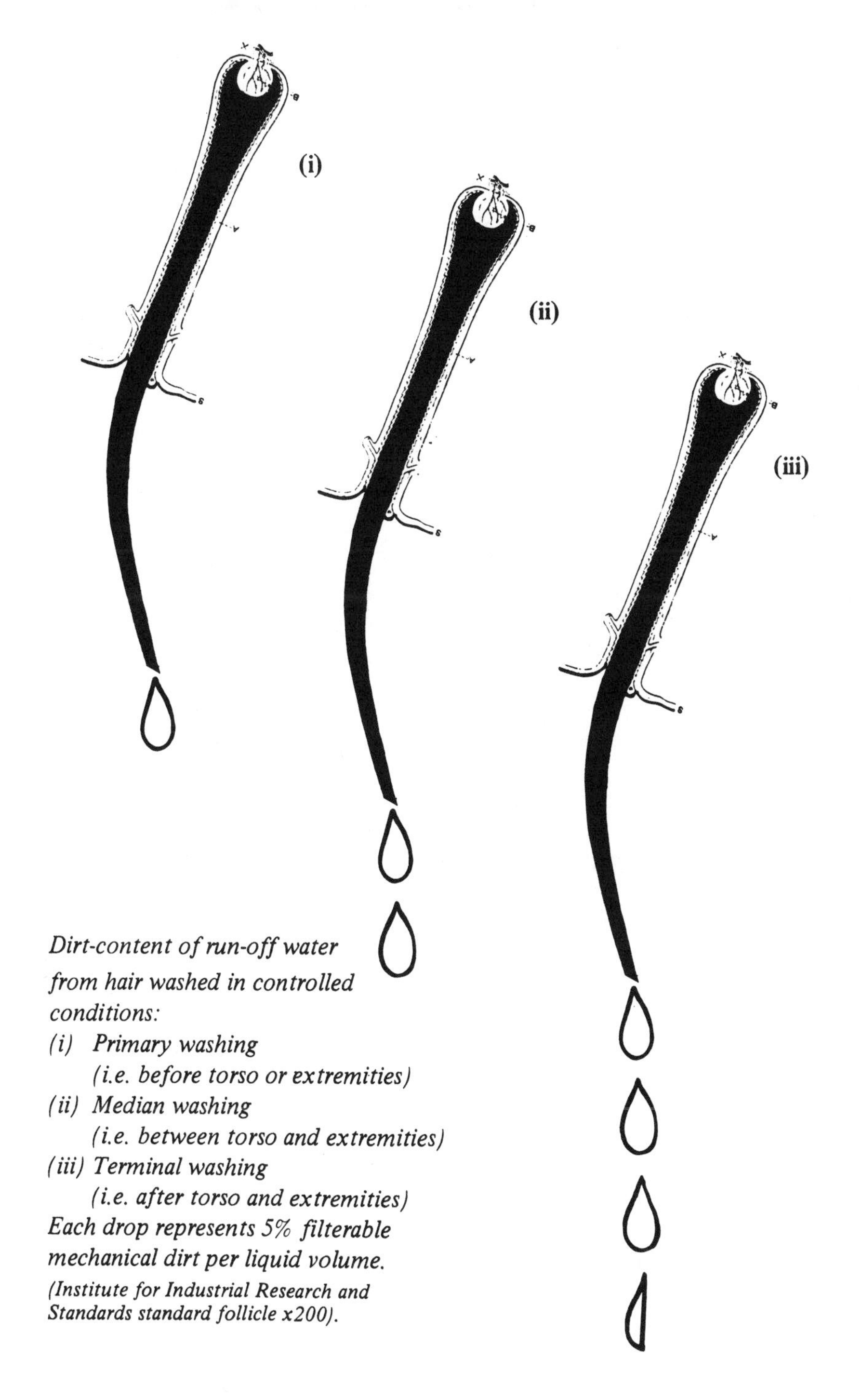

Dirt-content of run-off water from hair washed in controlled conditions:
(i) Primary washing (i.e. before torso or extremities)
(ii) Median washing (i.e. between torso and extremities)
(iii) Terminal washing (i.e. after torso and extremities)
Each drop represents 5% filterable mechanical dirt per liquid volume.
(Institute for Industrial Research and Standards standard follicle x200).

here? I was now leaning forward in the posture of one making a profound obeisance and when my hair had been sufficiently rinsed I raised my head slowly, allowing adequate time for run-off drainage. Paused thus with my head forward I again noticed the gleam in the rose window. The argument was clearly coming from that source. I peered in.

The girl was now frighteningly near. I was looking down at the spacious front hall of the hospital. She was standing at the doorway of the porter's glass-walled enquiry kiosk. The porter was gesticulating urgently towards a notice which announced visiting-hours. Her voice was shrouded in a cavernous gurgling and I could not discern the words spoken. The porter lifted a telephone hand-set and spoke briefly. Almost immediately a large nun arrived and further disputation with the girl ensued. She, however, was clearly one not easily rebuffed.

I heard the nurse at the door again, tapping loudly.

'Come now,' she said, 'If you can't manage better than that we'll have to give you a blanket bath in future.'

I knew the end was approaching and my hand dangled the fine chain connecting the centre of the overflow with the rubber plug in the vent-hole. There remained an opportunity to undertake one further experiment. Science had failed to establish the causes for the rotation of the whirlpool frequently noted around bath-vents. Many scholars held that the water should be expected to fall evenly over all points on the circular edge of the vent-hole, setting up a volume of immobile water exactly over the centre of the hole. Such immobile volume would presumably be in the form of an inverted cone and no-one had yet explained why this cone should prove so inherently unstable, falling constantly to one side or the other and setting up the whirlpool effect. And why should the whirlpool spin clockwise (if clockwise) or anti-clockwise (if anti-clockwise)? Was it, as some held, an effect of terrestrial axial rotation, differing with latitude, clockwise in one hemisphere, anti-clockwise in the other? Could human intervention alter whatever mysterious factors effect these tremendous cosmic movements.?

I chucked on the chain and the plug came up. A gathering rattle sounded in the drain-pipe as the water plunged down, but it was still too deep for any sign of a whirlpool. Clearly over

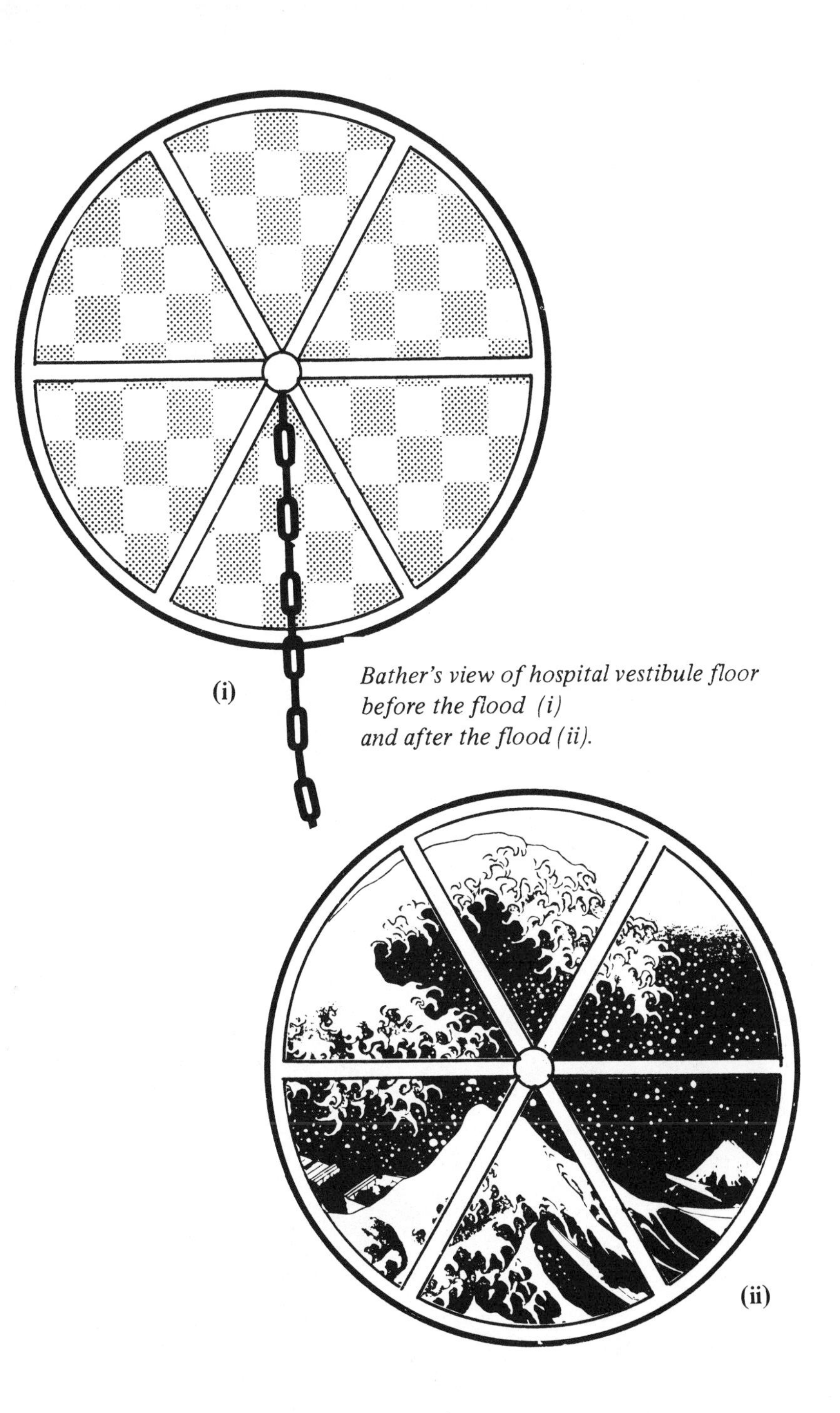

Bather's view of hospital vestibule floor
before the flood (i)
and after the flood (ii).

the deepening rumble I could hear the squeaking of the girl and the nun below, now raised to still greater volume and shrillness. I moved my head again towards the overflow and stared through it in amazement.

Great vertical rivers of water were plunging down on the hallway. Nun, girl and porter were buffeted and swirled about by the cascading torrents. Streaming freshets of sudsy grey effluent slopped about them, engulfing their feeble gestures of resistance in deluvian power. Surges of foam lapped about their feet, their knees, their waists. The black and white tiled floor disappeared in the grey depths. A watery vapour swayed over the flood and obscured the tearing vortex in which the three frail humans struggled ineffectually.

The nurse came in and clucked imperiously. 'Finished at last?' she said. 'I hope we did behind our ears.'

The whirlpool was clockwise.

Lip-top and end-wall overflow bathoscope by Wright, Sutcliffe and Son, Halifax, 1900. (Note dead-end overflow 0 and open-end vent-hole V).

3

You Drop Through that Transparent Air of Evening

Chaise Longue: a chair with support for the legs, *couch:* a bed or any place of rest; a lounge or sofa. *davenport:* a large couch or sofa, sometimes convertible into a bed. *divan:* a thickly-cushioned seat or sofa against the wall of a room. *lounge:* a sofa with a back and one raised end. *love seat:* double chair or small sofa seating two persons. *ottoman:* a cushioned seat or sofa without back or arms. *settee:* a long seat for several persons with a back. *settle:* a long high-backed seat or bench for several persons. *sofa:* a long stuffed couch or seat with raised back and ends.

CERTAINLY MORE THAN A CHAIR and less than a bed. Lightly stuffed and thinly cushioned. Long enough for two or perhaps three to sit rather tightly side by side. A back along half its length. One raised end. Perhaps a lounge but the word was unknown to the vocabulary of lower Drumcondra, where they speak the best English. Whatever the thing may have been I was reclining against its raised end and casually leaning an elbow on its part back. My feet were lying on its unraised end and one of them was in fact the reason for this inactive condition of the whole corpus. My right ankle was sore and mildly incapacitated.

My hands however were fit for duty and one of them was sidling gently along the fuzzy green velour in which the piece was upholstered. The fuzz was deeper and more satisfactory on unworn portions of the surface and in their search for fresher pastures my groping fingers slid gradually into the dark crevice between the back and the seat of the object. The tingling rub was now prickled with danger for who could know what razor-blades, needles, pins, thumb-tacks or rat-traps might not have been secreted here by time's erosion of things?

The forward-scouting finger froze suddenly as it touched something hard. Was this one of the old and rusted pieces of small hardware or haberdashery, injurious to the touch? It could inflict painful and lasting damage on a careless finger-tip. A slight pressure revealed that the item was not sharp at the end, while thin enough to indent only the central pad of the finger. Slipping cautiously over the end, the fingers encountered a smooth rounded surface extending for six inches or so along the bottom fold of the tucked-in velour. The farther end was lightly knurled. A ball-point pen?

I crooked one finger under the knurled end and raised it. Indeed the barrel of a ball-point pen. It contained no ink-laden cartridge and the knurled cap was easily removed. I blew through the tube and dislodged a few flakes of dried tobacco. I raised the tube to my eye and peered through it towards the window near which the lounge (sofa? couch?) was placed by a thoughtful host for the comfortable illumination of recumbent ankle-injured guests. The light from the window on the clear and shining smooth bore of the tube yielded a bright white circle at the centre of which the hard-edged far end of the tube outlined a green patch of the grass beyond the window.

I was vouchsafed an extraordinarily clear view of the grass-land and scanned about with my little penoscope. At the edge of the green I descried a small grove of trees with figures moving within it. Twisting the penoscope, I brought them into a sharp focus and saw a youth and a girl leaning their bicycles against a tree. They strolled off over the grass; I panned carefully with them, holding them in close-up and able even to hear their quiet murmur of conversation, sharp and clear as I rotated in the fingers of my free hand the detached knurled cap of my view-tube.

Suddenly the boy stopped and taking something small from a pocket exclaimed 'Will you marry me?' The girl burst into laughter, but a kindly laughter showing no surprise. The whole demeanour of the couple suggested that this proposal was no sudden passionate intensity but the formalising of an already-agreed relationship. 'Catch me first,' she cried and grabbing the tiny ring from his hand she ran away. He ran after her and just as he was about to grab her she stopped suddenly, turned and tossed the ring back in his direction.

He twisted in his lunge towards her in an attempt to catch it, giving a yelp of pain as his ankle gave under him and its supporting strength evaporated. He fell heavily, helpless and inadequate as she bent over him solicitously. He assured her he was alright except for the paralysing weakness of his right leg and held her hand for a moment. She kissed him quickly and lightly and stood up purposefully.

'O.K.,' she said, 'I'll straighten you out and go and ring my father. I know he's at home and he can drive over and collect you in the car. I'll have to wait at the gate to show him where we are but it shouldn't take more than a quarter of an hour or so.'

Gently and firmly she drew his damaged limb straight beside the sound one, tidied his clothes, put a rolled plastic raincoat from her saddle-bag under his head, kissed him again and with a last concerned look dashed off.

He was then in perfectly safe hands, even if they were for a quarter of an hour or so a half a mile away, and he had nothing to do but nurse his squashed vanity and bear the ache in his leg. The ring could not be far away, of course; he began examining the circular patch of grass at the middle of which lay his lumbar vertebra. The span of his outstretched arms was about five feet ten inches or so or one point eight six metres. The radius of the proposed circle was therefore about three feet, as near as dammit, the proposed area of exploration necessarily about twenty-two over seven by three in square feet say three by nine roughly about twenty-seven.

I took the penoscope from my eye and let my left hand delve again into the interesting fissure between the curving-down back of the lounge (sofa?) and its bulging seat. The fingers' next encounter elicited a tiny thrill of excitement as the hard flat cold disc it met could quite easily prove to be an interesting antique coin. I brought the object into viewing-range, held it close before my face. It was only a worn washer, originally forming part of the front hub assembly of a bicycle of relatively modern manufacture. I turned it over and over idly in my fingers and was surprised to notice through its circular centre the tiny figure of a man walking up the sky. How a man could walk up the sky and why he should do so were two things I could not understand.

I tossed the washer towards the fire-place, which it missed, and watched it roll along the edge of the fender until it came to rest falling finally and flatly over. I picked up the penoscope and squinted through to see how my man in the grass was getting on. I had some difficulty in picking him up and had to scan back and forth with some diligence, viewing, en passant, a few deer, a few goal-posts and a road-way with antique lamp-standards. Just as my eye lit upon my man I realised where he was: out on the Fifteen Acres.

I knew of course that the Phoenix Park is situated on one of the approach lanes for traffic into Dublin Airport and wondered could a helicopter perhaps be in flight somewhere so far up as to be out of sight while a man dangled in the sky from it at the end of a fine rope, far enough below to be within range of vision.

Grassman's quest in his green circle was proceeding no better than mine in the dim couch-canyon. He was examining with some disgust an object which in frontal elevation bore a superficial resemblance to an engagement ring.

Certain gaseous drinks, sealed in cans under pressure, are released to the lips of their drinkers by the removal from the top of the can of a tear-off strip. The tearing-off is achieved by the insertion of a finger in a ring of light non-ferrous metal which lies flat on the can-top. The lifting of the ring exerts leverage on a point at which it is bonded to the top (the exact centre in fact). The pressure of this leverage is assisted by the pressure of the gases within and the light rivet at the centre pops out. The ring may now be readily pulled off, taking with it a small strip of metal, roughly triangular in shape, which leaves an orifice in the top sufficient for drinking purposes.

Makers of the gaseous drinks in question, in an attempt to gain the goodwill of a discerning public, inscribe on the can the legend 'place ring in can avoid litter' but fail to address themselves to the larger problem of the disposal of the can itself. In fact many drinkers fail to observe the rubric and snapping away the tear-off strip proper insert one end of it in a tiny slot beside the rivet-mount which still adheres to the activating ring, and

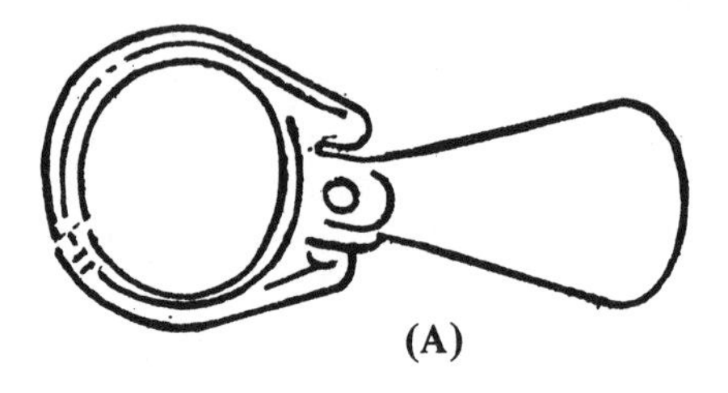

Detachable Ring and Strip, assembled.

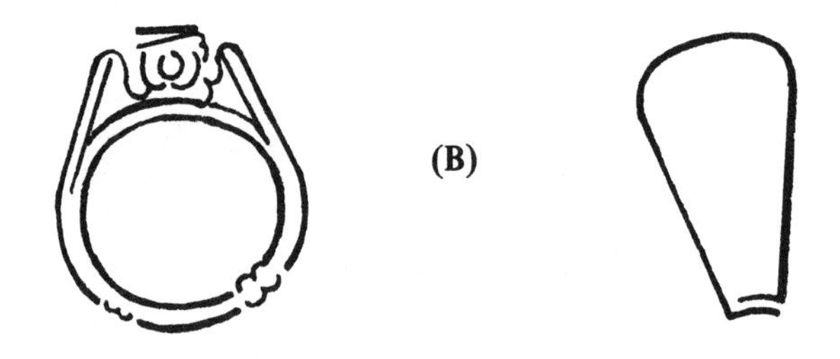

Detachable Ring and Strip, dismantled.

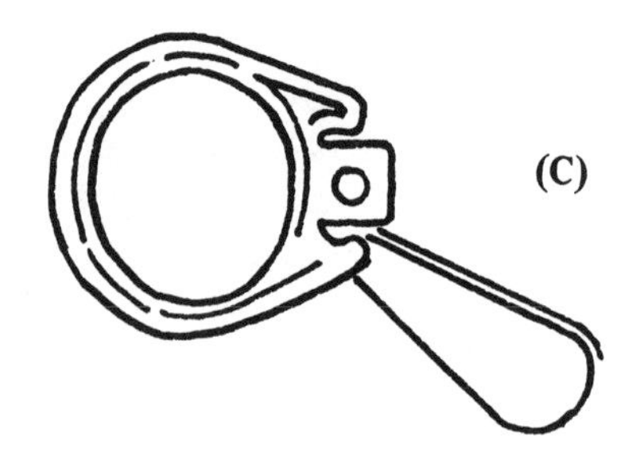

Strip inserted in Ring-Slot in preparation for launching.

by a judicious flick use the springiness of the strip to launch the ring on a highly satisfying flight as of a flying saucer. Hence it is that these dull rings of non-ferrous metal, their circularity impaired by a bulge in the rivet area as that of an engagement-ring is impaired by the setting of the precious stone, are to be found lying discarded in many places of public resort and in the recesses of sofas in rooms in which canned drinks have been consumed.

It was one of these rings his searching fingers had encountered and with doom-shaped inevitability mine found one too in their next forward movement, immediately undertaken.

He flicked the useless ring away, giving it a strong enough impulse to clear his proposed circle of exploration (thus, presumably, to avoid the waste of time which would be involved in rediscovering it). By happy accident the flying fragment of metal slipped on some appropriate current of air and glided gracefully in a gleaming arc for a perceptible moment before vanishing over the edge of peripheral vision. As I panned with it I saw on its tiny rim the golden gleam of the western-setting sun. When it disappeared, I saw in the vacant sky the pendant or sky-striding man, but a quick swivel up, down and across revealed no helicopter.

I slipped my hand back down into the furry glen and moved it along on its fingersome way.

Something small, hard, knobbly but not metallic. I lifted it and saw that it was a diminutive stamped-plastic model soldier or else a petrified jelly-baby. I had seen just such a model used as a toy deep-sea-diver. He was about an inch long and his feet were weighted so that immersed in water he would float neck-deep with his feet hanging correctly downwards. But in his feet there was also a small hole bored from below which contained a trapped bubble of air. Now, when pressure was applied to the top of the water, say by the depressing of a rubber membrane stretched across the top of the vessel, that pressure communicated itself to the little air-bubble tucked away in the feet and squeezed it smaller still. Smaller air-bubble, less buoyancy, diver sinks. Release pressure, air-bubble expands, more buoyancy, diver rises towards the surface. Nice adjustments of the pressure kept him drifting gently up and down, up and down, or held him in equilibrium at any desired level. Supposing the sky-strider were equipped with an analogous apparatus – a bag of lighter-than-air gas about the head and shoulders to keep him erect, a container near his feet containing another appropriate gas to be squeezed by a hand-operated lever and piston? Could he control his own level in the circumfluent air, sinking or rising or floating still?

Birds fly by flapping their wings up and down, but they can certainly stay successfully aloft without any apparent movement of their wings or other limbs. Perhaps the whole bird wavers slightly as he fixes himself on a suitable current and slides away along it at even height or rising and falling at will, side-slipping or drifting forward or even backward. I once saw two sea-gulls over the South Wall just beyond the Pigeon House where the Shelly Banks used to be, sailing with still wings in opposite directions on the same air-current.

Maybe the man upstairs had mastered the arcane art of the self-cancelling equilibrium of the air-currents and was held poised in mid-air by a freakish micro-climate.

I picked up the penoscope again and cast a quick glance at my man in the grass. His busy fingers were working away and with the elbow flexed he had reached a point a few inches from the side of his rib-cage. He scrabbled a few moments in the grass and picked up a small black tubular object which I was absolutely certain, with horrid foreknowledge, would prove to be the barrel of a ball-point pen. He brought it level with his eye and peered through it.

Raising my own penoscope I began to detect a strange synchronism between the actions of the man in the grass and mine. As he moved his little black tube skyward it seemed impossible to resist the conclusion that he too was examining Mr. Upstairs. I decided to put the matter to the test and swung my penoscope sharply to the left. As if connected by a rigid linkage his swung leftward too. Up too in even time with mine, down around, following a figure of eight, making a sharp crossing. I banked steeply but he hung on my tail, into a dive he came after me, up and over in a sharp loop with a roll off top, unerringly he stayed with me.

The last thing I saw as I dropped the thin tube from my eye was a samara from a sycamore-tree as it twirled downward on its double-scimitar wings of autumnal red and brown. It tipped his face gently as it went to earth.

Gliders are hauled into the sky by powered aeroplanes. Joined by a cord invisible to ground-bound viewers the two machines spiral upwards at a wonder-seeming evenness of distance apart. When the equally invisible upward thermal current buoys up the glider the invisible cord is slipped and plane and glider drift apart. The eye follows the effortless glider while the coarse mother-ship returns to earth. The glider spirals on up on the invisible stilts of the thermals until it too is lost to view.

Such thermals can be produced artificially. It is well known that the public lighting in the Phoenix Park is provided by interesting survivals of the pre-electric age – town gas lamps. Inflammable vapours are conducted to these outlets via subterranean tubes from the giant gasometers in the city and ignited duly at a fixed interval after sunset. The pale mantle-spread flame would be scarcely visible in bright sunlight but might through inadvertence or malfunction be left burning all day, inevitably, in such circumstances, generating a warm column of air ascending invisibly to the sky, there to press upwards invisible wings of finest transparent oiled silk mounted in a delicate framework of light rods hinged to the legs, arms, thighs and shoulders of the cloud-walker.

I whipped up the penoscope and directed it as well as I could towards the sky-man zone.

It did no more than spare my eyes the impingement of a number of rays of light from a variety of irrelevant quarters and allow them to react more energetically to light from his home district. Under these circumstances I was able to discern some traces of wings or wing-frames as posited above. It was, however, impossible to distinguish the aerofoil parameters clearly enough to decide whether it was in fact glider-style assembly or a form of kite. A man-carrying kite, or a kite-carrying man?

Your kite aerofoil is cunningly inserted into an air-current in such wise as to establish, by controlled turbulence, *over* its rear end a volume of air at lower pressure than is exerted by the volume of air *under* the same section, thus ensuring lift. The front of the kite must be held at such an angle that these counter-poised pressures are sustained to keep the assembly aloft; hence the importance of the earth-bound line attached to the kite-harness and controlling the angle of the aerofoil to the wind. I had already failed to detect any line which might be attaching my man to a stratospheric helicopter; I now similarly failed to detect a downward line shackling him to ground or pendant massy weight equivalent.

Grassman was doing a little gentle wiggling, perhaps to find a warmer patch of soil-contact for his back. In the process he moved his head and he was / I was / we were rewarded with a handsome view of the grass-scape of the Fifteen Acres. It seemed to stretch limitlessly from eye to horizon and was dappled with moving patches of glistening white where a faint erratic breeze curved the feathery blades of grass to catch the side-long glances of the sinking sun.

He was still near enough to the trees for the grass in his vicinity to have had some shelter from the day's sun and a few drops of earlier rain still adhered to nearby blades. An American writer, the late E. A. Poe, once discussed the strange case of an observer who had imagined he saw an immense monster tearing through the undergrowth of a distant hillside. It proved ultimately to be the magnified image of a tiny insect in the near foreground seen through the lens of an unnoticed droplet of clear water. Our case too? Search as we might, we could detect no animalcule within range.

If not a naturally magnified image, perhaps a contrived one. A greyish background of light diaphanous cloud as screen, a magic lantern of enormous luminosity to project, and some ingenious practical joker could hoodwink the population of north Dublin into believing a man was walking in the sky.*

If none of these explanations covered the blatant facts of the case, there could be an explanation in extra-scientific terms. The only person who enjoyed authority to walk extra-scientifically in the sky was the Archangel Gabriel and if it were he come to call the final court of appeal into session he was the only

* The Brocken spectre, a phenomenon observed in mountains, consists of a hugely magnified shadow of the observer cast by a low sun on clouds below the observer's level, sometimes doubled and sometimes surrounded by a rainbow-like coloured corona, but since both Grassman and I were at ground level it did not seem possible that we were witnessing this phenomenon and it was only later that the disquieting thought arose that we might have been no more than a double spectre in the eyes of the more favourably placed Skyman.

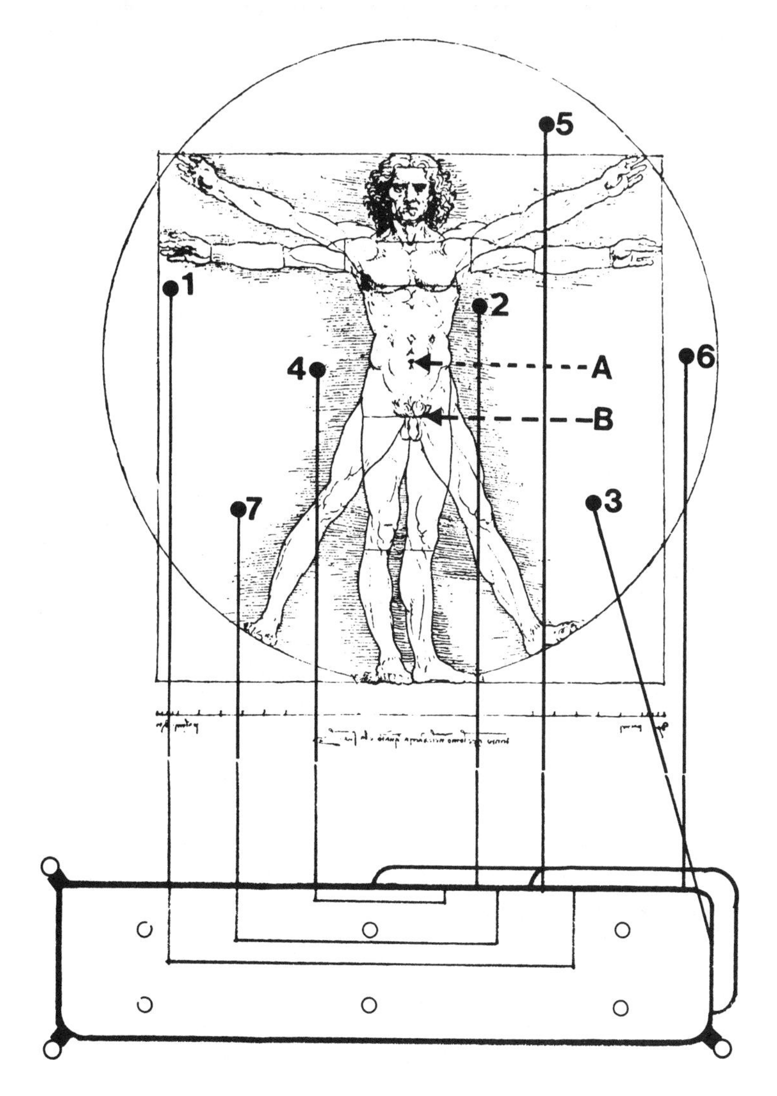

Record Grid of Finds at Fifteen Acres
(with projection to sofa-crevice)

A *Datum for circular orientation*
B *Datum for square orientation*

1 *Washer*
2 *Pen-barrel*
3 *Aerated-drink opening-ring*
4 *Stamped-plastic model soldier (petrified jelly-baby?)*
5 *Rusted ball-bearing*
6 *Neck of broken bottle*
7 *Lace-retaining eyelet*

visible sign that the day of wrath was at hand.

I heard a girl's voice calling, panting and concerned, as she and her father, who was smiling reassuringly, hove over the narrow horizon. They helped gently and the supine victim began to rise. The horizon spread and dropped dramatically around as the shoulders lifted and revealed a rim of distant housetops on the fringes of the Park. On one of them a high aerial was being erected and a skilful steeplejack was clambering busily hither and thither in an array of stays and guy-wires as he went about his proper business of securing the aluminium framework to the chimney-stack.

Between the trio and the road where the welcoming car was waiting there was one of the antique gas lamp-standards. Was it still in fact operational? Pausing in the hoist, he asked her would she shin up it and try a match near the surviving fragment of mantle. She exchanged a puzzled look with her father but complied. Standing on a flange protruding from the lamppost about three feet from the ground, she managed to insert in the lamp-housing an upreaching hand. She flicked the abrasive wheel of her father's lighter and the tiny spark was obliterated in an immense explosion which rolled flame and noise and terror around and over us all.

I recollect no further incidents worthy of notice in the evening's proceedings.

4

Natural Declension of the Soul at Night

I LAY QUIETLY AS BIDDEN, meditating on the stupidity of failing to look right, look left, before you cross the street, use your eyes, use your ears and then use your feet. On the other hand, perhaps it was not stupidity but the longitudinal thinness of the assailant bicycle which had caused this particular mishap. Mishap, certainly, and not catastrophe, for a broken nose is easily mended and coupled with general abrasions and slight shock insufficient to merit even a brief paragraph at the bottom of a column on an inside page in a local newspaper. Nevertheless the extensive bandaging was a nuisance, particularly the insistance that the hands be immobilised. 'Those little cuts could itch a lot as they heal and while you're asleep you might do yourself nasty damage by scratching.'

When I awoke, some hours later, unscratched, I opened my eyes and saw first a coarse-grained, ill-scanned reticule, sadly out of focus.

I had once seen my own eye, in a gross enlargement, without intervention of the normal process of vision. I was with a specialist for the checking of some minor ailment. He darkened the room and switched on his eye-examining machine, a point source of light set in the middle of a magnifying glass. This enabled him, by aiming the light through the translucent ball of my eye, to examine the back of the organ in some detail. From time to time as the fine ray passed back and forth it hit the optic nerve, without of course passing through the front lens of the eye as do most rays which impinge upon that nerve.

The fine ray, discreet as the aperture of a pinhole camera, focussed on the nerve the pattern of the blood-vessels through which it had travelled, and my eye – my brain? I? – sensed this as a monstrous vision, a huge bloody network of fine lines floating in the dark space of the consulting-room.

The grid now before me was less shocking and more transparent. It was possible to select one of the tiny interstices in the bandage and by peering through it to use it as some kind of peep-hole, however, inadequate, for getting at the world through the cocoon in which I was shrouded and mummied.

Through this peep-hole I could see her cycling slowly and I could recognise that she was on a quiet old suburban road with worn stone in the kerb and darkened yellow brick in the walls of the houses she passed. It was at a mean enough house she stopped, leaning her bicycle against the gate-pillar and passing through the narrow front garden. Small flower-beds, edged with lumps of rock, separated the path from little grass-plots thronged with flat clumps of daisies; the beds themselves were overrun by an invasive creeper with bulbous grey-green leaves, but all growth was stunted in winter torpor. Heaped fallaciously against the bottom of the house-wall were draggled stalks of sorrel, flaccid handfuls of dandelion-leaves, clippings of coarse scutch-grass, a foetid mess the gardener hoped would turn, by action of air, damp and self-generating warmth, into compost to enrich the earth.

She stood upon the doorstep, studying the paint-work of the door. Brass furniture had been heavily polished, with consequent removal of portions of adjacent paint. There had been indecision in the treatment of the furniture, some metal items had been painted over rather than polished. The paint on the broad leaf of the door itself had been subjected, while still wet, to gentle manipulation with a rubber comb alleged to impart the appearance of finest oak to the merest deal. Her eye soon alighted on the item she required, a brass lug fitted for working by finger and thumb. She gripped it firmly as its shape indicated and rotated it as rapidly as possible back and forth. Its central axle activated the clapper of a small bell within and the door was soon opened.

I once knew a dog, one of the Kerry Blue variety in large part at least. His owner took pity on the beast's apparent difficulties of vision, with shaggy hair constantly falling over the eyes, and neatly clipped the fringe. The dog immediately retired behind the lower fringe of a heavy velvet curtain until his own personal fringe regrew, the ignorant if well-meaning owner having meanwhile to deal with his pet's feeding and other physical necessities without the animal's being able or willing to leave his detached but indispensable eye-brow.

There was no dog behind the fringe of the velvet curtains I now beheld through my personal fringe of hospital gauze. The velvet was of a deep crimson hue, even deeper in the area of firm pile near its edge. A rope of brocade girded the curtain to the loins of a fake plaster pillar on the wall and held it in tasteful drapings, so tasteful indeed that they had not been altered for many years and dust had accumulated on exposed areas of all folds.

This curtain, together with a mate across the way, notionally divided the small hall-way in which she was standing into a front (or public, and distinguished strangers') area and a back

Devices (a) for examining gauze-enshrouded eye (b) the gauze-enshrouded image.

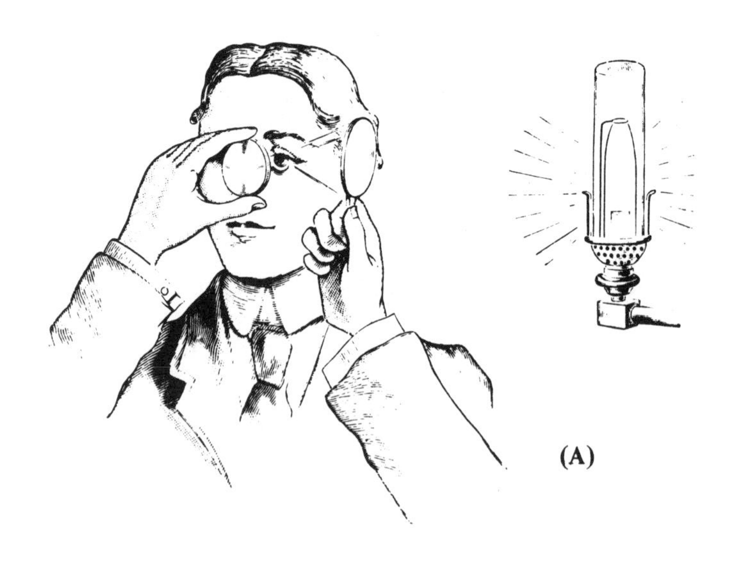

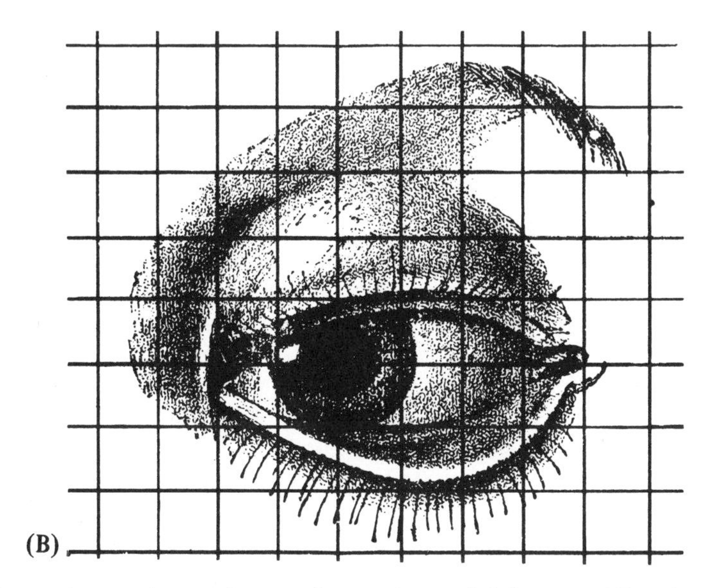

(B)

(or private, domestic, service and menials') area. The door to the drawing-room or front parlour was just forward of the curtains and as a blousy middle-aged woman with her hair in curlers showed the girl into the parlour, followed her in and closed the door, I closed my eyes.

The intense concentration necessary for peering through my gauze fringe without adverting to it had generated a latent image in my eye which developed only when my eye had been closed for a few moments. The fine white lines of the gauze were now a black outline against a fluorescent greenish-purple background. Here was a prime case for rubbing the eyes but the hands were immobilised 'in case you'd etc. etc.' and I had to wait for the eye itself to wear out the image through paler and paler reds and yellows until the original native lustrous black was restored.

Black, after all, is the natural undifferentiated state of things. I renewed the derision I had felt on hearing of the project of Soviet scientists who during the International Geophysical Year had bored into the earth's crust to carve out a fragment of the inner subterranean mantle. Miles upon miles they had dug, sending their probe deeper and deeper through alluvium, soil, subsoil, rock, down to the remote fastnesses approaching the boiling magma of the interior. Finally their bore had bitten successfully into the hard shell and brought up a neat round fragment of rock. They said it was greenish in colour.

Preposterous to imagine that greenishness had any meaning when applied to this detached piece of the inner layers of the earth, lying there quietly minding its own business for a million million years. Black was its only imaginable colour, unrelieved blackness. Did it then become greenish as it approached the surface? Or did it remain black and its steady scientific observers impute to it a foreign greenishness? Greenishness is only a state of my eye, striving to see through the thin gauze of my tegumental skin, my swaddling clothes and winding sheet. So indeed is blackness, merely the state of my eyes when not otherwise engaged, seeing, if only a single incident light ray were discreet enough, merely the private network of my inner eyeball.

I extruded the tip of my tongue beyond the lips cautiously and it touched – I touched? – an edge of the gauze bandage. It was finely serrated, its threads stiffened by some dressing and as it liquefied ever so slightly to the dampness of my tongue it distilled back to me, when I withdrew the tongue, a savour of hospitals. Smells and tastes, fluid and immeasurable, evoke more than the hard-edged abstractions of sound and vision, and smell is definitely the worse.

There was a special smell which attended some residences of the poorer classes I had once visited on behalf of a charitable organisation. Not given to attaching joyfulness or sorrowfulness to the levels of sensory stimulation, I attached no special point to this smell, beyond noting that it seemed to occur where there was overcrowding and little opportunity to wash clothes or the persons on whom they hung. I was to learn, sometime later, as I sat waiting to be served in a staff canteen.

A tiny insect stood on my waiting white plate. I was no stranger to tiny insects, having swatted many in the course of quiet reading in deck-chairs under summer trees. I flicked at him and he cracked, emitting a wave of pestilential vapour. Here was the smell I had known in the miserable homes of the poor, the double-distilled quintessential quiddity of human dirtiness. I knew nothing at the time of the manners and customs of the louse (it was a louse I had squashed) and only consultation with medical student friends revealed that he is (a) a parasite on the human and (b) of notable fecundity. Here, then, in his tiny grey body was concentrated the evolved total of unwashedness of clothes and their inhabitants; natural selection must have ensured the survival of the foetidest, through billions of foul generations to this grey fleck on my plate and beyond. Are there lice ever after?

There is something of the smell of the louse in all the effluvia of human activity, sweat, etc., etc. There was something of him, though only a tiny tang, in the front parlour, unwashed air lodging in the fibres of the worn carpet, a film of unwashed turf ash in the hearth, unwashed dust in the curtains, fall-out from the desiccated scent of generations of dried ladies.

When the eyes closed and the ears switched off except for the sad music of distant ear-drums, I was at liberty to consider the possibilities of using the other members and faculties. The hands, although immobilised ('in case you might, etc.') were capable of some internal movement and retained their tactile powers. I was confident that given sufficient time and training I could induce them to read for me materials prepared as literature for the blind. It would need of course the development of a machine to handle and dispense the Braille-pocked paper tape with some degree of remote control, so that a foot-activated machine could, over a length of approximately three quarters of my legs, supply reading matter to the fondling fingers and thereafter retrieve it continuously. But if my feet could be trained to drive such a machine could they not themselves be taught to read the Braille? Hence perhaps the dispensibility of certain upper members and the preservation of those of holy persons, as for example Francis Xavier and the native Lachtnan, separately from the rest of their bodies.

With such objects at his disposal, many of them preserved in handsome reliquaries, there seemed to be work available for some heavenly Frankenstein: two heads – Oliver Plunket's, if one insisted on using native materials, that of John the Baptist if one were prepared to admit an item imported from Amiens, France – several arms – those above-mentioned and one of Laurence O'Toole conserved in the parish dedicated to him on the north side of the city of Dublin – and even a tooth of the national apostle.

Dismemberment, however notional, I found distasteful and tried in my straitened circumstances to return to a contemplation of the integrated being. Two whole beings in fact for I had opened my eyes and there they were again at the other side of the gauze curtain.

–Oh, she's alright now, the older woman was saying, but I needn't tell you it's been really terrible. I mean to be feeling bad for so long and then not knowing if she should do anything about it, poor child, sure she couldn't know with her first, and when she did go to the doctor, it was the usual thing you know, oh you mustn't be worrying we'll just keep you quiet in here for a few days and everything will be alright, well, they sent her home after a few days and told her to stay in bed and she did of course but then she began to get these sort of crampy pains she said they were and I said, look, he'll just have to get in touch with that doctor again and so he did go down to the doctor and he said, well, alright, if you think it's getting urgent we'll see about getting a bed, but sure when he got home she was in an awful state again, really miserable and crying and all and getting these crampy pains all the time, so he knew he'd have to take her in without waiting for the bed or anything, I mean they must have some place for emergencies, but when he went to help her out of bed she caught hold of him and says 'no, no, there's something coming, don't move me, don't move me,' and they sort of froze there and then she went all limp, fainted I suppose and lay there real quiet and she was bleeding like mad all over the place it was terrible.

The eyes were tired again and I dropped the lids over them for recollection's sake. These twin membranes too were undoubtedly laced with a fine network of bloody lines, pulsing in synchronisation with the gentle thumping of my ears. One can direct or close the eye, not so the ear. Open twenty-four hours a day, seven days a week. In the depths of the night, when nothing else is available, your ear will keep you uselessly informed of the recurrent surge of your heart-beat, the swelling tide of nameless pulses about your body, hissing and whirring, now and then bursting into peaks of activity with clicks and pinging whines, telling you it's four bells in the staggered dog watch and all is well.

I had no wish to eavesdrop further on the conversation out there beyond the gauze curtain but could not help wondering what happened next. How are such things disposed of? The unfortunate girl, weak and gasping, wrapped in a blanket and a plastic sheet, carried clumsily downstairs, placed in a car, driven to a hospital, laid in a bed, sheet after drawn sheet taken from beneath her as she lay, the sheets red with clotted death, an embryonic eye here, there a blob of potential finger.

The casual experienced sister glances at the sheets, this for washing, that for destruction. Scalding water and man-eating detergent cleanse the one, the brown-muddied soup gurgles down the sink-hole, into the sewers, out to the pulsing sea, sinks peacefully to the littoral ooze to wait a million million years for the push of continents, the boiling volcanic surge from below, or perhaps the steady grind of a Soviet drill boring out round plugs of primal matter.

For the other, flame searing it to a curled, charred flake, a hiss of tiny jets of released gas, an oily roll of smoke over a chimney, dissipated into the vanishing sky.

For the bigger lumps, a more considerate treatment. Not consecrated ground, obviously out of the question, but maybe a small neat box, a reliquary if a humble one, paraded in seemly fashion before the hatted men in the graveyard, directed courteously towards the perimeter, lifted over the hedge, placed discreetly in a small hole, covered hastily but respectfully with the hard lumps of yellow clay.

I surfaced briefly, flicking open an eye just in time to see the girl saying goodbye.

Each arm, leg, member must have a central indispensable core. The intense studies I had carried out during the day had shown me how peripheral was some of the soft-wear – muscles, nerves – with which the extremities were so generously endowed. The bandaging of eyes, ears, nose, mouth, hands had not prevented me from functioning in a fairly normal fashion. The assembly of the essential cores of the members then would leave me something like a matchstick man, running jerkily across the margins of flicked pages in thick schoolbooks. Peripherals in such a case are eight matches, the central core the longest and ninth, with an outline loop of head at the top, a couple of dots for the eyes.

Reduced to such dimensions I should have to abandon the interesting project for hand-to-toe Braille and the head on its stick body would look suspiciously like the weapon of the medieval fool, a bladder on a rod. Only the black dots of the eyeholes would remain and I fearfully set about unlidding these again.

It must have been late evening in that quiet old suburb for nothing was to be seen in the dark behind the trace of gauze which still floated before me. It was confused now with its own after-image and could have been a white grid on a black background or a black grid on a white background, the one cancelling the other and the two tending towards zero. For a while lustrous greens and reds glowed there, shot through with the netted blood-vessels on the consultant's wall, but the whole faded and left me singularly alone, biologically degraded like the unconsecrated blood-stained ooze on the ocean floor.

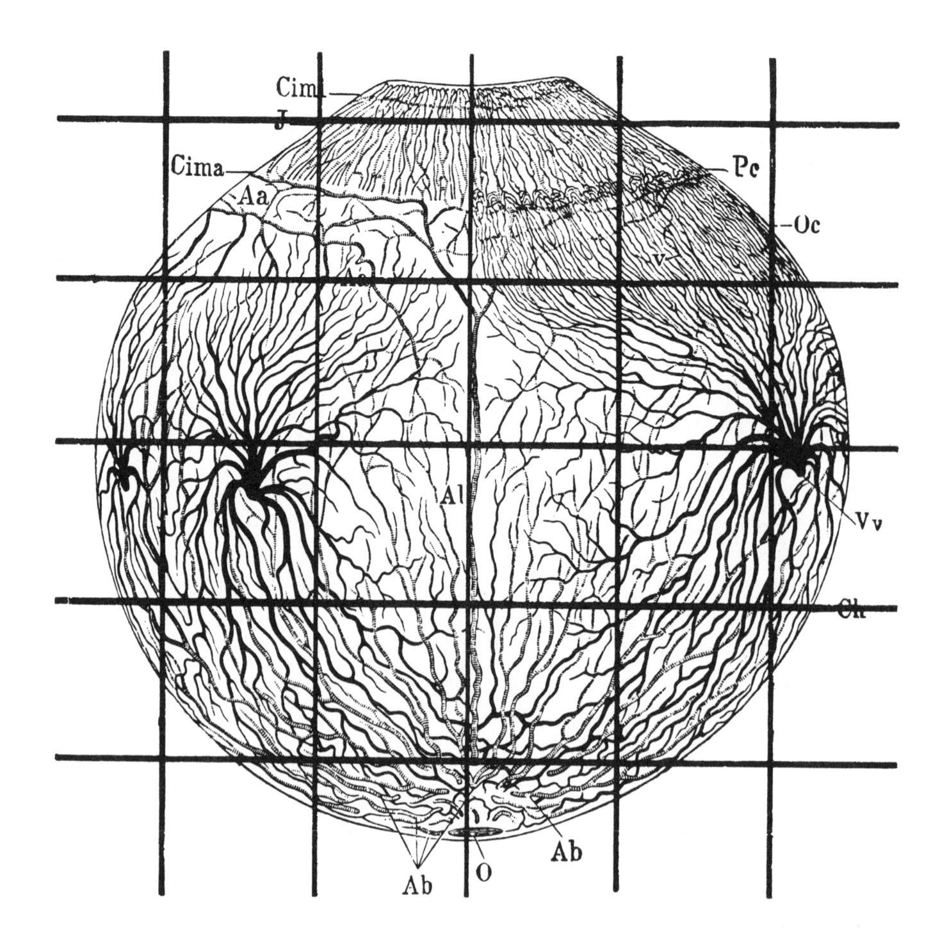